W9-BEN-397

The Little Red Hen
(Makes a Pizza)

The Little

RETOLD BY

Philemon Sturges

ILLUSTRATED BY

Amy Walrod

ReD HeN (makes a Pizza)

PUFFIN BOOKS

To the ducks, the cats, the furry dogs, and especially to
the beautiful Red Hen at Studio Goodwin-Sturges—P.S.

To John, with love and thanks,
and thanks to Philemon—A.W.

PUFFIN BOOKS
Published by the Penguin Group
Penguin Putnam Books for Young Readers,
345 Hudson Street, New York, New York 10014, U.S.A.
Penguin Books Ltd, 80 Strand, London, WC2R ORL, England
Penguin Books Australia Ltd, 250 Camberwell Road, Camberwell, Victoria 3124, Australia
Penguin Books Canada Ltd, 10 Alcorn Avenue, Toronto, Ontario, Canada M4V 3B2
Penguin Books (N.Z.) Ltd, 182-190 Wairau Road, Auckland 10, New Zealand
Penguin Books Ltd, Registered Offices: Harmondsworth, Middlesex, England

First published in the United States of America by Dutton Children's Books,
a division of Penguin Putnam Books for Young Readers, 1999
Published by Puffin Books, a division of Penguin Putnam Books for Young Readers, 2002

13 15 17 19 20 18 16 14

Text copyright © Philemon Sturges, 1999
Illustrations copyright © Amy Walrod, 1999
All rights reserved
CIP Data is available.

ISBN 0-525-45953-7
Puffin Books ISBN 0-14-230189-2

Manufactured in China

Except in the United States of America, this book is sold subject to the condition that it shall not,
by way of trade or otherwise, be lent, re-sold, hired out, or otherwise circulated without the publisher's
prior consent in any form of binding or cover other than that in which it is published and without
a similar condition including this condition being imposed on the subsequent purchaser.

T he Little Red Hen had eaten the
last slice of her tasty loaf of bread. She'd sipped
a cup of chickweed tea and taken her nap. Now she was
hungry again. So she scratched through her cupboard and
spied a can of tomato sauce.

Why don't I make a lovely little pizza? she said to herself.

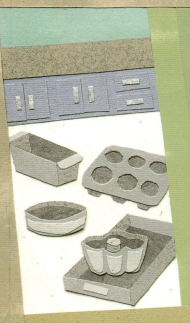

She rummaged through her pan drawer. There were bread pans, cake pans, muffin pans, frying pans—all kinds of pans—but not one single pan was large and round and flat.

"Cluck," she said. "I need a pizza pan."

She stuck her head out the window. "Good morning," she called. "Does anybody have a pizza pan?"

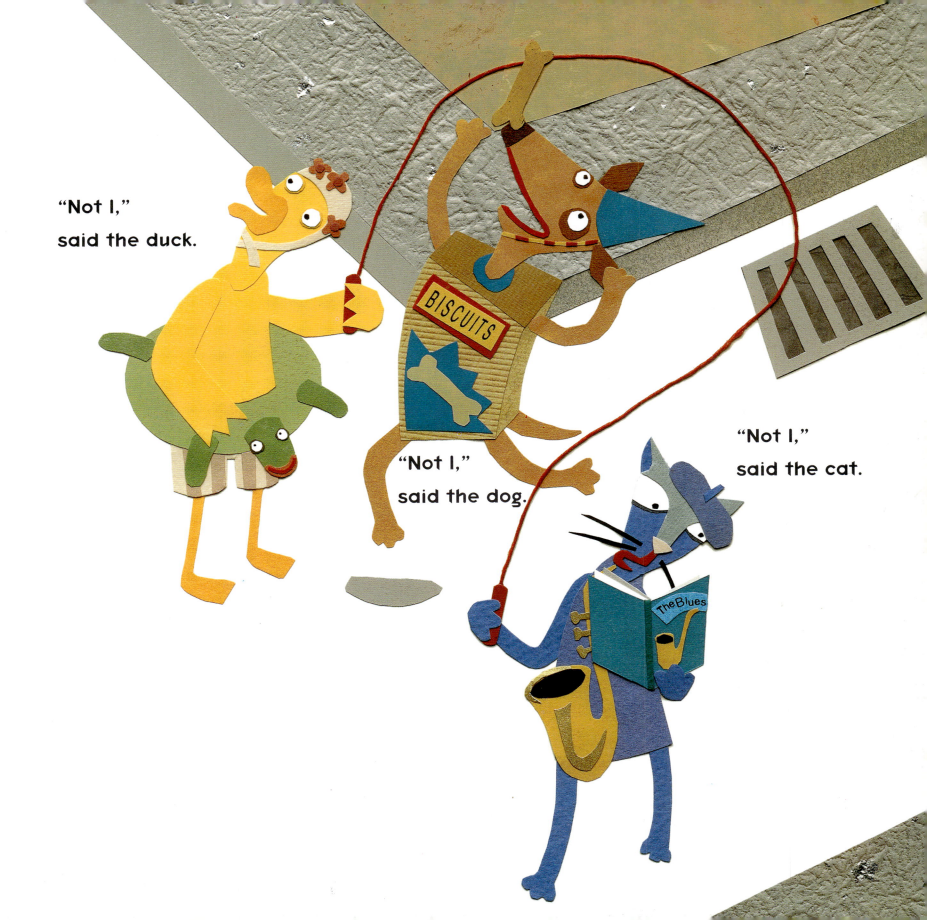

"Very well, then, I'll fetch one myself," said the Little Red Hen. So she went to the hardware store. She bought a pizza pan, a large mixing bowl, a pizza slicer, and . . . some other stuff.

THE DO IT YOURSELF GUIDE TO sink installation (and other things)

hand's best friends

nails

super suds

PLANT food

When she got home, she opened the cupboard.

She saw beans and rice,

sugar and spices,

jars of jam,   and jars of honey,

and even pickled eggplant
—but no flour.

"Cluck," she said. "I need flour."

She stuck her head out the window. "Hello," she said.
"Who'll run to the store and get me some flour?"

"Not I,"
said the dog.

"Not I,"
said the cat.

"Not I,"
said the duck.

"Very well, then, I'll fetch some myself," said the Little Red Hen.
So she went to the supermarket. She bought some flour, some
salt, some oil, and . . . some other stuff.

When she got home, she opened the fridge.

"Cluck," she said. "There's cream cheese, blue cheese, string cheese, and Swiss cheese . . . but no mozzarella!" So . . .

She stuck her head out the window. "Excuse me," she said. "Who will go to the store and buy me some mozzarella?"

"Not I," said the duck.

"Not I," said the dog.

"Not I," said the cat.

"Very well, then, I'll fetch some myself," said the Little Red Hen.

NOW SERVING 7

serv-o-matic

So the Little Red Hen went to the delicatessen. She bought

some mozzarella, pepperoni, and olives;

mozzarella

black olives

some mushrooms, onions, and garlic;

a can of eight small anchovies;

Anchovies

and . . .

Chocolates

some other stuff. But no pickled eggplant.

JOE

SUPER savings ON PICKLED EGGPLANT

When she got home, the Little Red Hen put on her apron and stuck her head out the window. "Good afternoon," she said. "Who will help me make some pizza dough?"

"Not I," said the duck.

"Not I," said the dog.

"Not I," said the cat.

"Very well, then, I'll make it myself," said the Little Red Hen.

So she put the flour and some other stuff into her mixing bowl and stirred and mixed and mixed and kneaded and kneaded and pounded until she had a big ball of pizza dough.

After the dough rose, the Little Red Hen rolled it flat and folded it and rolled it again and spun it around her head several times.

When the dough was just right, she tossed it way up in the air
one last time for good luck and put it in her pizza pan.

Then she stuck her head out the window. "Excuse me," she said. "Who will help me make the topping?"

"Not I," said the duck.

"Not I," said the dog.

"Not I," said the cat.

"Very well, then, I'll make it myself," said the Little Red Hen.

So she chopped and grated and grated and sliced. Next she opened her can of tomato sauce and spread it all over the pizza dough. On top of that, she put some grated mozzarella, some sliced pepperoni, some chopped olives, some mushrooms, some onions and garlic, eight small anchovies, and . . . some other stuff. But no pickled eggplant.

The Little Red Hen looked at her pizza. It looked just right. She put it in the oven and sat down to sip a cup of chickweed tea.

Pretty soon a delicious smell drifted from the oven. It filled the room and floated out the window.

My lovely little pizza must be ready, she thought.

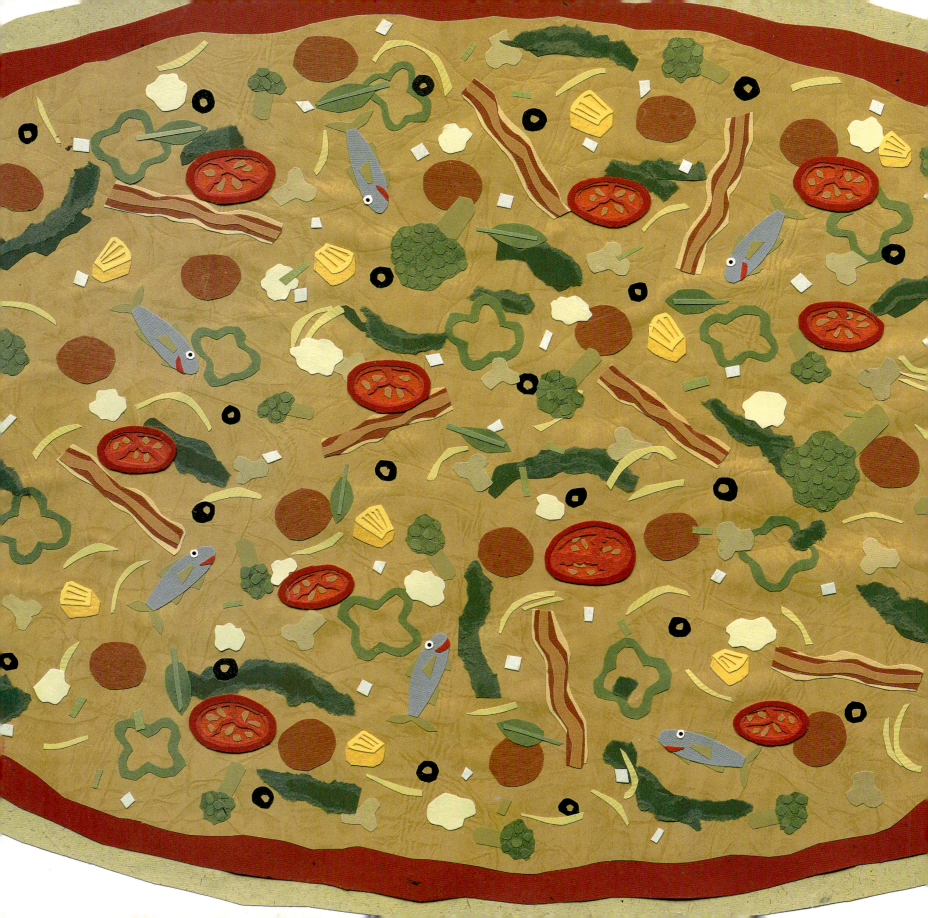

It was lovely, but it was not little.

So she stuck her head out the window. "Good evening," she said. "Would anybody like some pizza?"

It was lovely, but it was not little.

So she stuck her head out the window. "Good evening," she said. "Would anybody like some pizza?"

Can you guess what the duck said?

Can you guess what the dog said??

Can you guess what the cat said???

They all said, "YES!" of course.

(But the cat scraped most of the topping off his share!)
When the pizza was all gone, the Little Red Hen made herself
another cup of chickweed tea.

Then she asked, "Who will help me do the dishes?"
Now can you guess what the duck, the dog, and the cat each said?

dream vacations

They each said,

"I will."

And they did.